ABC come and SKANK with me

A–Z Reggae Legends

Written by Karimah Campbell

Printed in the United Kingdom

A CIP catalogue record for this book is available from the British Library.

ISBN: 978-1-7391458-0-4

Cover and Interior Art by Janine Carrington janine.carrington@gmail.com

The artist references and lyrics are provided for educational purposes. Please support the artists by purchasing related recordings.

Auntie Annette,

Without your tapes and records, I wouldn't have an appreciation for these legends.

Thank you x

A
Alton Ellis

He was still in love with you, which made him so very happy.

B

He wanted to rule his destiny, so travelled over hills and valleys. He could go on and on - the full story has never been told.

Buju Banton

He came with love and not hatred. Goodness and mercy followed him all the days of his life.

Dennis Brown

Gregory Isaacs

The night nurse wanted to be his number one. But he wanted to know her future plans.

Half Pint

He was a superstar and not a substitute lover.

I Roy

He felt the pain from the first cut because it was the deepest.

Jimmy Cliff

He could clearly see that you could get it if you really wanted, and taught one and all that the harder they come, the harder they fall.

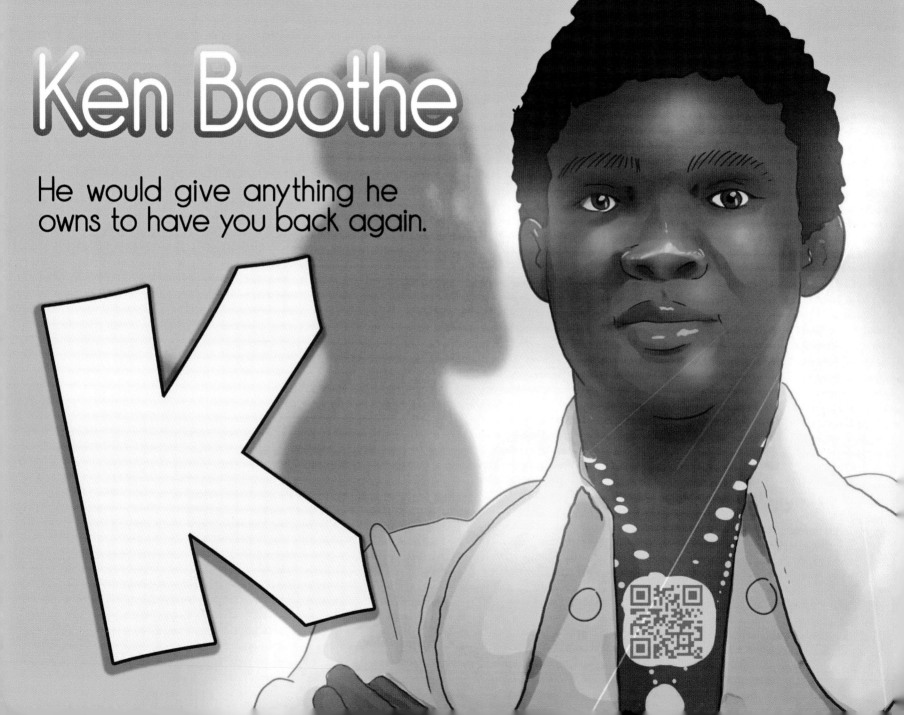

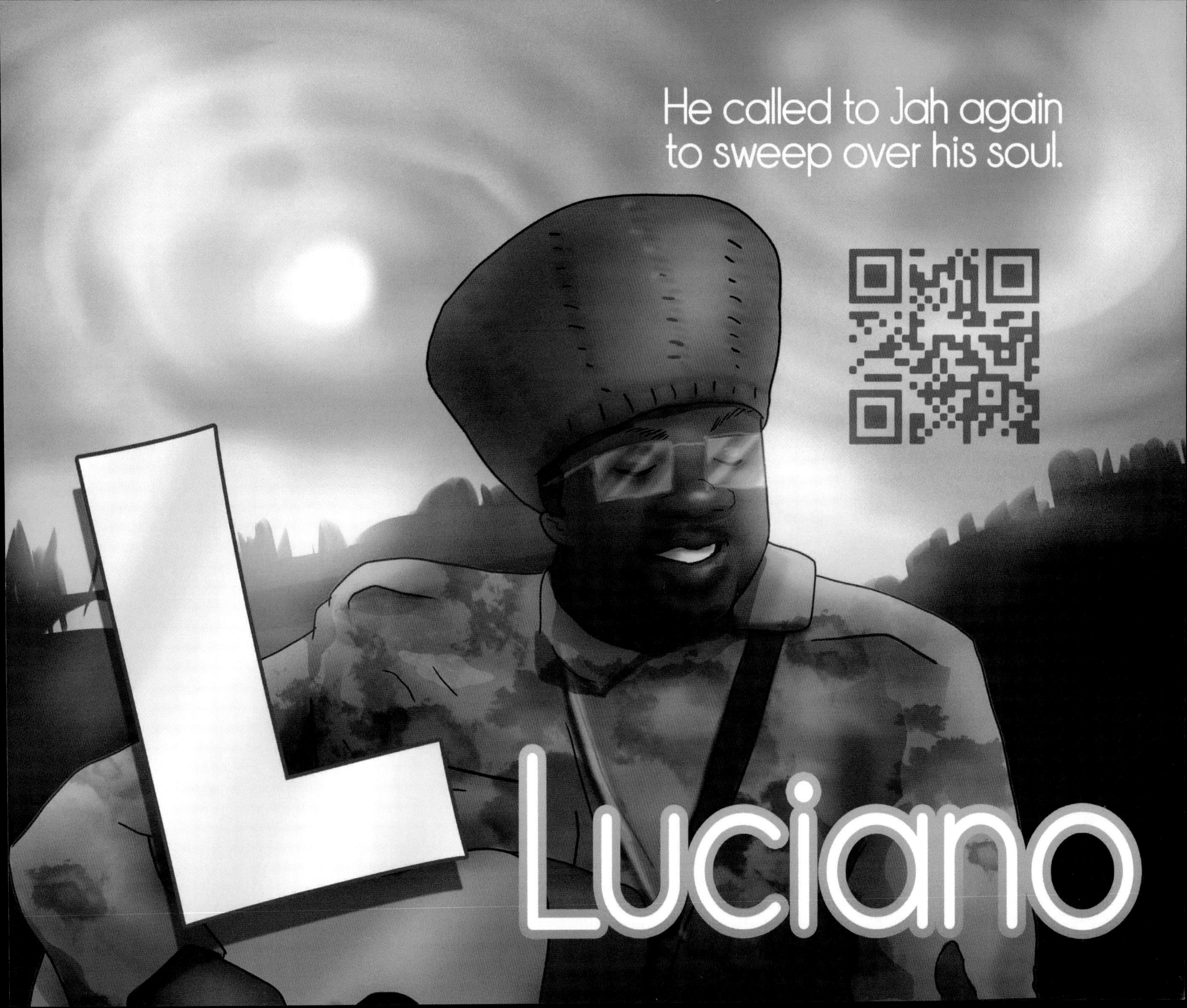
He called to Jah again
to sweep over his soul.
L
Luciano

M

Marcia Griffiths

She taught the world
what it means to be
young, gifted and Black.

Ninjaman

Took us to Jamaica Town, the land of his birth.

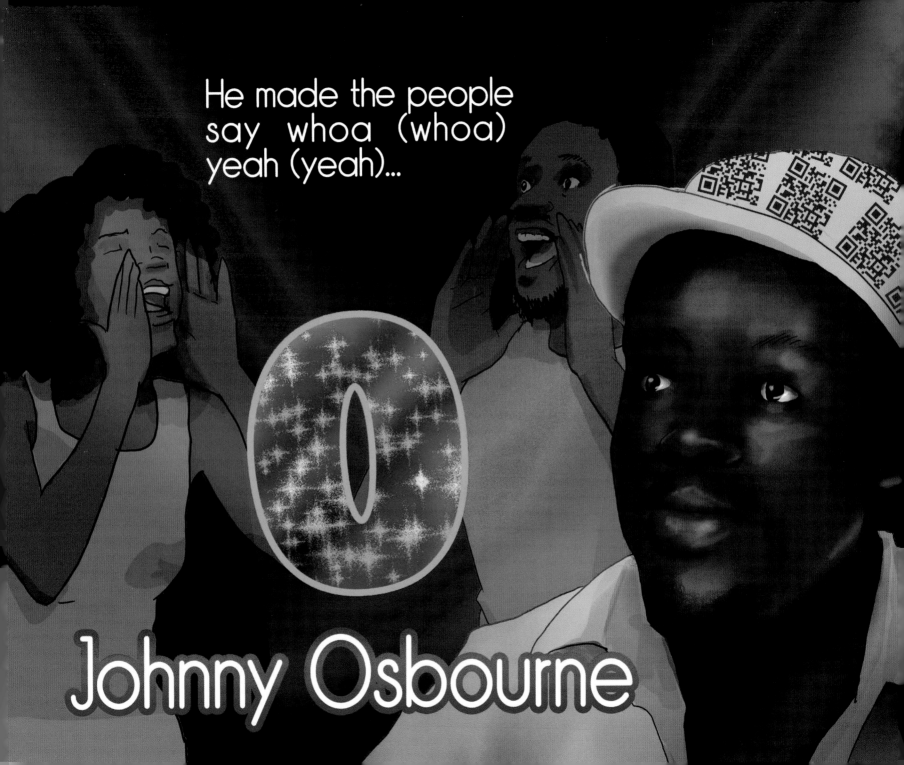

Queen Ifrica

A true lioness on the rise , warned those feeling like a badman to keep it to themselves.

Richie Spice

He loved the girl and was not shy.
Maybe it was her brown skin,
her dimples, or the angel in her eyes.

Sugar Minott

He had a good thing going.

Taurus Riley

Seeing the natural beauty in Black Queens, he told the world that she's royal.

U-Roy

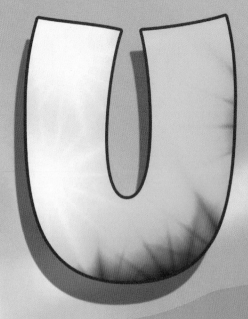

He's a rebel, a soul rebel. He's also a capturer, a soul adventurer.

Vybz Kartel

Everybody asked him where he got his Clarks.

The Wailers and Bob Marley

They had us all getting up, standing up for our rights.

eXcitement

Is the feeling you get when you hear reggae music.

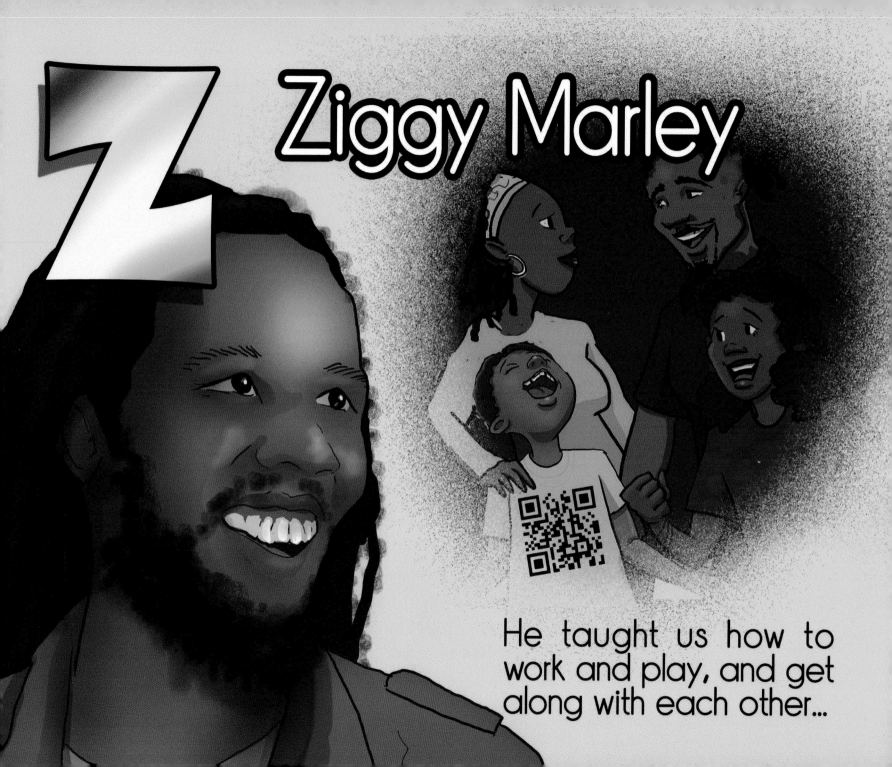

About the Author

Karimah Campbell is a writer and technologist of Jamaican descent from South London. Listed in the Financial Times Top 100 Black and minority ethnic leaders in technology, Gifted and Black and Black Tech Queens' founder Karimah Campbell has a true passion for seeing Black people of all ages represented, and reaching their full potential.

Her first book, "ABC Come And Skank With Me", was inspired by the musical blood running through her veins and her passion for keeping her rich culture alive through generations.